A Letter from Acheron . . .

Hola, mi amigos,

It's broad daylight and I'm up after an all-night session of chasing the Daimon menace—something that never makes me happy (the up all day with no sleep part, not the killing Daimons part—I actually enjoy the latter).

As I was stalking the Daimons last night, I happened upon another bookstore with one of "those" books in the windows. Damn. Just when you think you're safe, some human discovers your existence. And if that's not bad enough, she then starts to write about it and publish it! I don't know who this Kenyon person is, but she's way too close to the Dark-Hunters for our own good.

How does she know so much about us? I went to her Web site and there was even more leakage. But you know the old saying, if you can't beat them, join them. With all that speculation abounding, there are some who have it right and some who have it wrong. The wrong ticks me off even more than the right. So with that in mind, here's a little something to help those who need a small primer about our world.

—Acheron Parthenopaeus

New York Times
Bestselling Author

Sherrilyn
Kenyon

*invites you deeper
into the world of the Dark-Hunters...*

St. Martin's Paperbacks

DARK-HUNTER SAMPLER

Copyright © 2005 by St. Martin's Press, LLC.

"Second Chances" copyright © 2005 by Sherrilyn Kenyon.

Glossary copyright © 2005 by Sherrilyn Kenyon.

ISBN: 0-312-93853-5

Printed in the United States of America

St. Martin's Paperbacks edition / July 2005

St. Martin's Paperbacks are published by St. Martin's Press, 175 Fifth
Avenue, New York, NY 10010.

10 9 8 7 6 5 4 3 2 1

Contents

Second Chances

A shiver of déjà vu crawled down Ash's spine as he walked along an eerie, fog-filled hallway he'd hoped to never see again. The nether realm of Tartarus was reserved for those who were being punished in the afterlife for crimes committed in a human lifetime.

The screams of the damned echoed off walls as black as Ash's own soul. He had to give Hades credit—the ancient Greek god definitely knew how to make people suffer.

At moments like this, Ash hated being a god. It was unbearable to know he had the power to stop and change things, and the profound responsibility to let nature take its course. Human free will should never be altered. His own damnation was a constant reminder of exactly why.

Still, the reality of it ate at him constantly. How he envied Artemis, Hades, and many of the other gods who could shrug off human suffering as par for the course.

But having once been human, Ash wasn't immune to it. He understood what caused people to make the bad decisions they would spend the rest of eternity paying for. And that human part of himself wanted desperately to ease their pain.

It was a bittersweet gift his mother had given him when she had made the decision to hide him in the human world. To this day he wasn't sure if he should thank her or curse her for it.

Today, he wanted to curse her.

"You don't have to do this."

He ignored Artemis's voice in his head. He did have to do this.

It was time.

Ash stopped at a doorway that was covered with an iridescent slime. It shimmered like a rainbow oil slick in the dim light. To his surprise, there was no sound coming from inside. No movement. It was as if the occupant were dead.

But unlike the others who lived in Tartarus, this particular person couldn't die.

At least not until Ash did, and since he was a god . . .

He used his powers to open the door without touching it.

It was completely black inside the small, dingy room. Horrifying images of his human past slammed into him at the sight. Long-buried emotions ripped at him with daggers of pain that lacerated his heart.

He wanted to run from this place.

He knew he couldn't.

Grinding his teeth, Ash forced himself to take the six steps that separated him from the man who was curled into a ball in one corner. An identical replica of himself, the man had long blond hair that was snarled from the time he'd spent here without brushing it.

But then, Ash never willingly wore his hair blond. It was a wretched reminder of a time in his past that he wanted his damnedest to forget.

The man on the floor wasn't moving. His eyes were clenched shut like a child who thought that if he made no sound, no moves, the nightmare would end.

Ash had lived a long time in just such a state, and like the man before him, he had prayed for death repeatedly.

But unlike his own prayers, which had gone unheard, Styxx's would be answered.

"Styxx," he said, his low tone echoing off the walls.

Styxx didn't react.

Ash knelt down and did something that had disgusted Styxx when they had been human brothers in ancient Greece. He touched his brother's shoulder.

"Styxx?" he tried again.

Styxx screamed as Ash broke through the brutal memories of horror that Mnimi, the goddess of memory, had given to Styxx as punishment for trying to kill him. It was a punishment Ash had never agreed with. No one needed the memories of his human past.

Not even him.

He could hear Styxx's thoughts as they left Ash's past and returned to Styxx's control.

Knowing his brother would be repulsed by him, Ash let go and stepped back.

As humans, he and Styxx had never been close. Styxx had hated him with an unreasoning passion. For his own part, Ash had aggravated that hatred by deliberately provoking him.

Ash's human rationale had been that if they were going to hate him anyway, then he would give them all good cause for it. He'd gone out of his way to repulse them. Out of his way to antagonize them.

Only their sister had ever given him kindness.

And in the end, Ash had betrayed her . . .

Styxx struggled to breathe as he became aware of the fact that he wasn't Acheron.

I am Styxx. Greek prince. Heir to . . .

No, he wasn't the rightful heir to anything. Acheron had been. He and his father had stolen that from Acheron.

They had taken everything from him.

Everything.

For the first time in eleven thousand years, Styxx understood that reality. In spite of what his father had convinced him, they had greatly wronged Acheron.

The Greek goddess Mnimi had been right. The world as Prince Styxx had seen it had been whitewashed by lies and by hatred.

The world of Acheron had been entirely different. It had been steeped in loneliness and pain, and decorated with terror. It was a world he'd never dreamed existed. Sheltered and protected all his life, Styxx had never known a single insult. Never known hunger or suffering.

But Acheron had . . .

His body shook uncontrollably as Styxx looked around the dark, cold room. He had seen such a place in Acheron's memories.

A place they had gleefully left Acheron to face alone. Only this place was cleaner. Less frightening.

And he was a lot older than Acheron had been.

Styxx covered his eyes and wept as the agony of that memory tore through him anew. He felt Acheron's emotions. His hopelessness. His despair.

He heard Acheron's screams for death. His silent pleas for mercy—silent because to voice them only made his situation worse.

They echoed and taunted him from the past.

How many times had Styxx hurt him? Guilt gnawed at him, making him sick from it.

"I'll take them away from you."

Styxx flinched at the voice that sounded identical to his own, except for the soft lilting quality that marked Acheron's from the years he had spent in Atlantis.

Years Styxx wished to the gods that he could go back

and change. Poor Acheron. No one deserved what had been handed to him.

"No," Styxx said quietly, his voice shaking as he gathered himself together. "I don't want you to."

He glanced up to see the surprise on Acheron's face.

It was something Acheron hid quickly behind a mask of stoicism. "There's no reason for you to know everything about me. My memories have never served anyone anything but pain."

That wasn't true and Styxx knew it. "If you take them from me, I will hate you again."

"I don't mind."

No doubt. Acheron was used to being hated.

Styxx met that eerie swirling gaze of his levelly. "I do."

Ash couldn't breathe from the raw emotions he felt as he watched Styxx push himself to his feet.

They were so much alike physically and yet polar extremes when it came to their past and their present.

All they really had in common was that they were both longed-for heirs. Styxx had been born to inherit his father's Greek kingdom while Acheron had been conceived by an Atlantean goddess to destroy the world.

It was a destiny neither of them had ever fulfilled.

To protect Ash from the wrath of the Atlantean gods who wanted him dead, his true mother had forced him into the womb of Styxx's mother and then tied their life forces together to protect Ash. Ash had been born human against his will . . . and against the will of his human surrogate family, who had somehow sensed he wasn't really one of them.

And they had hated him for it.

"How long have I been here?" Styxx asked, looking around his dark prison.

"Three years."

Styxx laughed bitterly. "It seemed like forever."

It probably had. Ash didn't envy Styxx having to suffer the memories of Ash's human past. Then again, he envied himself even less for having lived them.

He cleared his throat. "I can return you to the Vanishing Isle again, or you can stay here in the Underworld. I can't take you into the Elysian Fields, but there are other areas here that are almost as peaceful."

"What did you have to bargain with Artemis and Hades for that?"

Ash looked away, not wanting to think about it. "It doesn't matter."

Styxx took a step toward him, then stopped. "It does matter. I know what it costs you now . . . what it cost you then."

"Then you know it doesn't matter to me."

Styxx scoffed. "No. I know you're lying, Acheron. I'm the only one who does."

Ash flinched at the truth. But it changed nothing. "Make your decision, Styxx. I don't have any more time to waste here."

Styxx took another step forward. He stood so close now that Ash could see his reflection in Styxx's blue eyes. Those eyes pierced him with sincerity. "I want to go to Katoteros."

Ash frowned. "Why?"

"I want to know my brother."

Ash scoffed at that. "You don't have a brother," he reminded him. It was something Styxx had proclaimed loud and clear throughout the centuries. "We only shared a womb for a very short time."

Styxx did something he had never done before. He reached out and touched Ash's shoulder. That touch seared Ash as it reminded him of the boy he'd been who had wanted nothing more than the love of his human family.

A boy they had spat on and denied.

"You told me once, long ago," Styxx said in a ragged tone, "to look into a mirror and see your face. I refused to then. But now Mnimi has forced me to look at my own reflection. I've seen it through my eyes and I've seen it through yours. I wish to the gods that I could change what happened between us. If I could go back, I would never deny you. But I can't. We both know that. Now I just want the chance to know you as I should have known you all those centuries ago."

Angered at his noble speech and at a painful past that no mere handful of words could ease, Ash used his powers to pin him back to the wall, away from him. Styxx hovered spread-eagle above the floor, his face pale as Ash showed him his powers. He could tell by Styxx's thoughts that he was aware of exactly what he could do. Even though they were linked together, Ash could kill him with a single thought. He could shred him into pieces.

Part of him wanted to. It was the part of him his human family had turned vicious. The part of him that belonged to his real mother, the Destroyer.

"I am not a god of forgiveness."

Styxx met his gaze without flinching. "And I'm not a man used to apologizing. We are linked. You know it and I know it."

"How could I ever trust you?"

Styxx wanted to weep at that question. Acheron was right. How could he trust him? He'd done nothing but hurt his brother.

He'd even tried to kill him.

"You can't. But I have lived inside your memories for the last three years. I know the pain you hide. I know the pain I caused. If I stay here, I will go mad from the screams. If I return to the Vanishing Isle, I'll languish there alone and in time I will probably learn to hate you all over again."

Styxx paused as grief swept through him at the truth. "I don't want to hate you any more, Acheron. You are a god who can control human fate. Is it not possible that there was a reason why we were joined together? Surely the Fates meant for us to be brothers."

Ash looked away as those words echoed in his head. It was a divine cruelty that he could see the fate of everyone around him, except for those who were important to him or those whose fates were intertwined with his own. He held the fate of the entire world in his hand and yet he couldn't see his own future.

How screwed up was that?

How unfair?

He looked at his "brother." Styxx was more likely to skewer him than he was to speak to him.

And yet he sensed something different about him.

Forget it. Erase his memory of you and leave him here to rot.

It was kinder than anything Styxx had ever done to him. But deep inside, down in a place that Ash hated was that little boy who had reached out for his brother. That little boy who had cried out repeatedly for his family only to find himself alone.

Should Ash deny that boy, too?

He set Styxx back on the ground.

Ash didn't move as memories and the emotions they reawakened assailed him. He could sense Styxx was approaching. He tensed out of habit. Every time Styxx had ever drawn near, he had hurt him.

"I can't undo the past," Styxx whispered. "But in the future, I will gladly lay my life down for you, brother."

Before he realized what Styxx was doing, Styxx pulled him close.

Still Ash didn't move as he felt Styxx's arms around

him. He'd dreamed of this moment as a child. He'd ached for it.

The angry god inside him wanted to shatter Styxx into pieces for daring to touch him now, but that innocent part of him, that human heart . . . shattered. It was the part that he listened to.

Ash wrapped his arms around his brother and held him for the first time in their lives.

"I'm so sorry," Styxx said in a ragged tone.

Ash nodded as he pulled away. "To err is human, to forgive divine."

Styxx shook his head at the quote. "I don't ask for your forgiveness. I don't deserve it. I only ask for a chance to show you now that I'm not the fool I was once."

Ash only hoped he could believe it. The odds were against them both. Every time Styxx had been given an opportunity to assuage their past, he had used it to hurt him more.

Closing his eyes, Ash teleported them out of Tartarus and into Katoteros, the realm that had once been home to the Atlantean gods.

Styxx pulled back to gape at the opulent foyer where they stood. Everything was white and crisp, almost sterile. "So this is where you live," he breathed, awed by the beauty.

"No," Acheron said as he folded his arms over his chest, and indicated the tall, gilded windows that looked out over the tranquil water that stretched toward the horizon. "I live across the river Athlia, on the other side of the Lypi Shores. There is no Charon to ferry you across the river to my home so don't bother looking."

Styxx was completely confused by that. "I don't understand."

Acheron took a step back from him, and Styxx was

puzzled by the suspicion he saw in his brother's silver eyes. "I will see to it that you have servants and all you could ever desire here."

"But I thought we were going to be together."

Acheron shook his head. "You made your choice. You wanted to come here, so here you are."

But this wasn't what he wanted. He'd thought . . .

Styxx tried to approach him only to find himself cut off by an invisible wall. "I thought you said to err is human, to forgive divine."

Those swirling, silver eyes burned into him. "I'm a god, Styxx, not a saint. I do forgive you, but trusting you is another matter. As you said, you shall have to prove yourself to me. Until then, you and I shall take this one step at a time and then we will see what is to become of us."

And as soon as those words were spoken, Styxx found himself alone.

Q & A with Sherrilyn Kenyon

First things first: How are the Dark-Hunter books different from everything else out there?

These aren't your mama's vampires. They're unlike anything that has ever come before them. Born from my imagination and years of research, the Dark-Hunters are truly unique. I've never been the kind of person who treads the well-worn path of others. I'd much rather find my own way. So with machete in hand, I reexamined the folklore and myths of the vampire and created my own take of how they came into being. Whereas traditional vampires are innately evil, mine can be, but their vampirism doesn't come from an evil source per se. It comes from the deep desires of a race that just wants to live a little longer. Fighters and warriors who don't want to lie down and die because some ancient god cursed them for something their ancestors did. I took the vampire world and reworked it with a new set of rules and laws. I wanted something that would be uniquely mine, something that would surprise the reader in every book so that the story and characters would never grow stale in the retelling.

How did you first think of the Dark-Hunters?

I started the series back in the mid-1980s when I "met" Acheron and based several short stories on him and the vampire hunters he ran with. From there, the Hunters, as they were then called, stayed with me and I worked on them in between other projects. They are a culmination of my lifetime of interest in vampires and history. The very first Hunter stories were written while I was attending Georgia College, in Milledgeville, Georgia. I wrote the very first Acheron short in Room 222 of Wells Hall.

Speaking of history, your heroes come from a bewildering array of times and cultures. How much research do you do and how do you keep track of them all?

I always laugh whenever someone asks me how I keep track of them. How do you keep track of your family and friends? The Dark-Hunters are as real to me as my family is. I live with them constantly and those details are stored in the same place in my brain as my sons' shoe sizes, clothing sizes, and eating preferences. My best friend often calls me the idiot savant of all things DH. I think that's why I can't remember where my car keys or shoes are on any given day. My brain is too cluttered with DH facts.

As for the research, most of the Dark-Hunters come from the time periods I am intimate with: ancient Rome and Greece, the Middle Ages and such. The other Dark-Hunters are areas that I researched a lot in college. I was lucky to have been born with a tremendous curiosity. Plus, I've kept up with a lot of friends who are now teaching various topics. If there's something I can't find, I ring them up and ask.

Wow. And that must partially explain your knowledge of the Greek gods. Can you give us some details on why you chose Artemis to be the goddess of the Dark-Hunters?

She was a natural since she is goddess of the hunt and is associated with Selene, who was the goddess of the moon. Not to mention her twin brother, Apollo, is the god of the sun and of plagues. If you are building a world about a race of people who have been banished from daylight, who better than Apollo to pick on? It was only natural, after he cursed his race to prey on mankind, that his twin, who was goddess of the hunt, would be the one to set up another race to control and kill those who were hurting humans.

But more than that, there are hundreds of different legends and stories written by the ancient Greeks and Romans that often contradict each other. Each ancient writer took a god or goddess and a story and made it their own. Artemis and Apollo were gods of many facets and faces. All the gods were. Apollo is both the god of healing and the god of plagues. Artemis is the goddess of childbirth and is said to have shot her arrows into the bellies of mothers who are laboring, to kill both mother and child. These writers portrayed their gods as being very human with all human foibles.

I have always loved the complexity of the ancient gods. Take Ares, for example: the all-powerful god of war, and yet you often find him in myths where he is being bested by mortals and at times he's even shown as a crybaby. Ancient writers didn't shirk from making their pantheon real. We see ourselves in the gods. It's why I love Artemis so much. She's complex and highly unpredictable. I never know what she's going to do.

Okay, now tell me about the Atlantean pantheon—did you make them up yourself or is there source material for them somewhere? Where do you find your inspiration for the Atlantean gods' stories?

Since Atlantis is a mythological place that has yet to be proven to exist, I took quite a lot of liberties with it. I love Hesiod and I have always admired his *Theogony*. I spent hours as a child reading and rereading it. I found the origin stories of the Greek gods fascinating and I wanted to create something every bit as complex and gripping. I wanted to build my own world. The story of the Atlantean pantheon is totally my own. I started with the premise, what if Atlantis was real? Who would have been their gods if not the Greeks? What stories would they have told? What caused their empire to crumble? If I were an ancient writer, how would I have explained their origins and death? And I built my world from there. One day I want to write my own *Theogony* for the Atlanteans.

Bad boys are a recurring element in your novels. I'm thinking especially of Zarek from *Dance with the Devil*, who actually siphons gas from a motorcycle into his mouth to spit on a fire. Where do you get your knowledge of bad boys and the crazy things they do?

That has to come from the lunatics I was raised with (sorry, guys). I love the guys in my family, but they are definitely a different breed. You know, they think duct tape really is a bandage and a cure for, oh, everything— ironically enough, modern medicine has proven that it will cure warts. (See, Buddy, you were right and I admit it.) So they may be vindicated yet.

Every time I turned around, one of them was doing

something remarkably weird and foolish. As a child, my official job was to call for the ambulance whenever they got hurt . . . which was often. They are the kind of guys who hook jumper cables to power lines just to see what will happen (I really wish I were making that up). Or set fire to themselves while having a blue flame contest (again, I wish I were that imaginative). Case in point, my brother called a few days ago complaining about one of the guys who was in his garage where he keeps his race car and racing fuel (this is the most flammable fluid on the planet). He looks up and the guy is actually smoking while working on the car. They have never recognized danger.

When will we get Acheron's story? Will his book be the last in the series?

No, Ash won't be the last book of the series. At first I was going to make his book the halfway point, but I decided that would be too cruel to the readers who are dying for his book. Look for his story in the next few years. The final book of the series is a surprise and it is already planned out. In fact, significant keys to that story have appeared in already published books and more will appear in books to come. But I haven't written it yet and I hope that I won't write it for a very long time to come.

You also have strong female Dark-Hunters—*Seize the Night* is the first book to really feature one—some of whom are Amazons. How much do you identify with them, since you grew up surrounded by males?

They are their own unique people. I'm not sure if I "identify" with any per se. I guess because I was around so many guys, I've always been a take-charge kind of person and I respect that in all people, male or female.

How did you get started writing?

I've always been a writer. I came out of the womb, literally, wanting to do this. In my Brownie manual, it has scrawled, "When I grow up, I want to be . . ." and I wrote, "A writer and a mother." I wrote my very first novel when I was seven and I published my first piece when I was in third grade. I made my first professional sell at age fourteen. Over the years, I wrote and published everything from horror to science fiction/fantasy to poetry to romance to nonfiction.

Because I've always wanted this, I'm basically a workaholic who spends anywhere from thirteen to twenty hours a day writing. It's what I live for.

You obviously put that kind of work ethic into every aspect of your writing—your Web site is amazing. Where do you get the energy to keep it up-to-date, and do you do it all yourself?

I have a couple of helpers who tweak for me, but it is primarily my baby. I play on the site every day, and much like a museum, you only see a percentage of what's there. I have many more pages that are under development at all times that I'm constantly tinkering with.

The Dark-Hunter presence in the chats and on the bulletin board is one of my favorite aspects of the Hunter-Legends.com experience. How does that work?

The "live" Dark-Hunters are friends and family who have graciously volunteered their time to role-play. The only thing they have in common with the characters are their names, and maybe a few of the more annoying personality traits . . . They know basic Dark-Hunter information, but not all details of their characters have been revealed to them.

And finally, speaking of fantasies, is Sanctuary a real place?

Oh, how I wish. Believe me, if Sanctuary were real, I'd be parked on a bar stool ogling Dev and the guys in New Orleans, and not in my little room writing the books. The only place Sanctuary exists is in my mind. And no, it's not based on any real bar in New Orleans. Sorry. If you look up the address 688 Ursulines, you'll find a convent there. That address was chosen for two reasons. One, it pays tribute to my favorite punk bar in the 1980s: 688, which was on Spring Street in Atlanta. And two, I wanted an address that didn't exist so that people wouldn't show up at someone's house in the French Quarter looking for the Peltiers. The Dungeon, however, is real and on Toulouse Street (and if you're over twenty-five, wear ear plugs—it's really loud there).

Glossary

Abadonna: Atlantean term of honor. Means "the heart of the destroyer."

Act of Vengeance: In exchange for their souls, Artemis allows all new Dark-Hunters to have twenty-four hours to exact revenge on those who wronged them in their human life. After the twenty-four-hour period, they belong to her and are trained by Acheron.

Adelfos: Greek for "brother."

Agrotera, Katra (Kat): She is handmaiden to both Apollymi and Artemis and serves as a bodyguard to Cassandra Peters. She has a mysterious affinity for Acheron, and is known as the Abadonna. In *Seize the Night*, Artemis releases her from her service in order for Apollymi to help Acheron.

Agrotera is also one of the Greek names for Artemis, meaning "strength" or "wild hunter."

Akelos Daimons: A branch of Daimons who have taken an oath to kill only the humans who deserve it—murderers and criminals.

Akra: The Atlantean term for "lady and master."

Akri: The Atlantean term for "lord and master."

Akribos: Greek endearment meaning "dear" or "precious."

Alastor: A demon who sometimes works with the Were-Hunters to cause mischief. Conjured in *Night Play* by Vane's mother, Bryani, to bring Bride back in time to Dark Age Britain.

Alexander, Grace: A down-to-earth psychologist, Grace has the fortune (or misfortune) to count psychic Selena Laurens as a best friend. She is the wife of Julian Alexander and heroine of *Fantasy Lover*. And yes, both she and her husband are immortal.

Alexander, Julian: An ancient Greek general who trained and fought alongside Kyrian of Thrace (and was originally his commanding officer). He is a demigod who was cursed by his half-brother Priapus to become a sex slave. Julian is now the husband of Grace Alexander and a professor of classics at Loyola and Tulane. He is an Oracle, and the hero of *Fantasy Lover*.

Alexion: Atlantean word meaning "defender."

Ambrosia and Nectar: Food and drink of the gods. Consuming them will make a mortal into an immortal demigod.

Anaimikos Daimon: A Daimon who feeds only from another Daimon in order to drain him.

Apollites: Apollites are a race created by the Greek god Apollo. More beautiful and stronger than mankind, they were blessed with psychic abilities. Apollo loved his people and wanted them to replace mankind. They were sent to Atlantis where they intermarried with the Atlantean natives. Until the day that the Apollite/Atlantean queen, in a rage of jealousy, sent her people to kill Apollo's Greek human mistress and his son. In retaliation, Apollo cursed his people threefold:

1. Because they made it appear that an animal had killed his beloved, they would have to feed off each other's blood in order to live. They were given fangs and the eyes of a predator.

2. They could never again walk in his daylight realm.

3. On their twenty-seventh birthday (the age his mistress was murdered), they would all disintegrate slowly and painfully over a twenty-four-hour period until they were dust. (See also **Daimons.**)

   Today many of them blend seamlessly into the human world while others live in segregated communes.

Apollymi: An Atlantean goddess known as "the Great Destroyer." Protects and uses the Spathi Daimons and keeps an elite group of around thirty Illuminati as her guards, in addition to Charonte demons and ceredons. She is Archon's wife and Apostolos's mother. For centuries, she has been trapped in Kalosis where she can see the human world and other gods, but not affect them. However, she can still control the Charontes.

Apostolos: The son of Apollymi. He is the Harbinger who will bring about the end of the world.

Arcadians: See **Were-Hunters.**

Archon: Atlantean counterpart to Zeus. He is the son of Chaos, who first established order throughout the universe his father had created. Mate of Apollymi. Also called Kosmetas, which means "orderer." He is the one who ordered the death of Apostolos and who trapped Apollymi in Kalosis.

Aristo/Aristi: A rare breed of Arcadian with the ability to wield magic effortlessly. They are the most powerful of their kind. Aristi are considered gods in the Arcadian realm and are guarded zealously by patria who would gladly die for them.

Artemis: The redheaded, passionate Greek goddess of the hunt, and creator of the Dark-Hunters. She has twin obsessions with Acheron Parthenopaeus and her own comfort.

Astrid: Astrid is the daughter of Themis, and the sister of the Three Fates. She is a Justice Nymph, an immortal impartial judge who is sent down to earth to rule on possible rogue Dark-Hunters. Olympian justice states that once accused, the defendant must prove himself worthy of mercy. Since the gods only accuse with good cause, Astrid has only been called in to judge guilty Dark-Hunters, and she is beginning to give up hope that there are any innocents. She is the heroine of *Dance with the Devil* and married to Zarek of Moesia.

Atlantis: An ancient island nation with an advanced culture and its own pantheon of gods. It sank into the Aegean Sea eleven thousand years ago.

Atropos: Oldest of the Three Fates, responsible for cutting the threads of lives. Daughter of Themis and sister to Astrid. Also known as Atty.

Blood Rite Squires: The Squires called out to hunt rogue Dark-Hunters or to execute humans/Squires who betray their world. They are all marked with a spiderweb tattoo on their hands.

Blue Blood Squires: Squires who come from a family with many generations of Squires.

Bolt-holes: Portals between Kalosis and the human world, often used by Spathi Daimons to escape Dark-Hunters. Also known as laminas.

Brady, William Jessup: See **Sundown.**

Callabrax: Spartan or actually Dorean (the ancient precursors of the Spartans) Dark-Hunter. One of the first three Dark-Hunters created by Artemis, along with Kyros and Ias.

Callyx: An Apollite who seeks vengeance against Zarek for his wife's death in *Dance with the Devil*. The most recent incarnation of Thanatos.

Camulus: A Gaulish god of war, forced into retirement. Wants to reclaim his godhood.

Carvaletti, Otto: Half Italian mafia, half Blue Blood Squire, with a Ph.D. in film from Princeton. He has a black spiderweb tattoo over the back of his knuckles. Now assigned to Valerius in New Orleans, where he often pretends to be a stupid, loudly dressed lout to annoy his boss.

Ceredon: A creature with the head of a dog, the body of a dragon, and the tail of a scorpion. Several of them protect Apollymi.

Charonte demon: An ancient type of demon that the Atlantean gods managed to tame. Fearsome, powerful, all but unstoppable, they can bond to gods, Hunters, or humans as companions. Once bonded, they can rest in the form of a tattoo on their bonded's body. Charontes are all appetite—they love to shop, kill, and eat everything. They are very easy to annoy and very dangerous when angry. Simi is Acheron's bonded Charonte, and like a daughter to him.

Clotho: One of the Three Fates who is in charge of spinning the threads of lives. Daughter of Themis and sister of Atropos, Lachesis, and Astrid. Also known as Cloie.

Corbin: Born an ancient Greek queen, Corbin was married and widowed young. She fought to keep her husband's throne as her own, and was a beloved queen. Her reign was uncontested until her brother-in-law made a pact with a barbarian tribe to sack the city and burn it to the ground. She died trying to save her servants and their children.

Cronus: Greek god of time.

Cult of Pollux: Apollites who take an oath to die exactly as Apollo cursed them to die—to neither commit suicide nor turn Daimon.

Daimons: Daimons are Apollites who refuse to die at age twenty-seven. They have to steal human souls to artificially elongate their life span. However, once a human soul is taken it begins to die, leaving Daimons always looking for their next victims. So long as they have a living human soul within them, they can continue to live indefinitely. Any Apollite who takes a human soul into his or her body is classified a Daimon.

D'Alerian: Oneroi Dream-Hunter, son of Morpheus, he is a healer and helper to the Dark-Hunters. D'Alerian is a straight man who never met a rule he didn't love. He keeps a constant vigil over the Dark-Hunters and is quick to step in with aid whenever one of them needs it. He and Acheron are close friends.

Dark-Hunters: Dark-Hunters are immortal warriors created from those who died wrongfully. Whenever such a person dies, the soul screams out for vengeance. The strongest and angriest of the screams echo through the halls of Olympus. Whenever one reaches Artemis, she considers offering a deal to the one who screamed:

Give her your soul, agree to fight the Daimons who are trying to kill and enslave mankind, and she will make you immortal.

Once the bargain is struck, the new Dark-Hunter is branded with Artemis's double bow-and-arrow logo and allowed an Act of Vengeance. He or she trains with Acheron Parthenopaeus, the enigmatic leader of the Dark-Hunters, and is assigned a location on earth. The Dark-Hunter then spends the rest of eternity fighting Daimons and other evil. Like the Daimons they kill, they have fangs, light-sensitive eyes, and a prohibition against going out in the daylight. The only things that can kill a Dark-Hunter are sunlight, beheading, or total dismemberment. Those who have read *Dance with the Devil* also know that piercing the bow-and-arrow mark can kill them as well. It's something Acheron keeps from them since he doesn't want them to panic and concentrate on it while they're fighting. To do so would give that knowledge to the Daimons who would have a very easy way to kill them.

Artemis pays them well for their services, and provides them with human helpers. (See **Squires**.)

The only way for a Dark-Hunter to become free of Artemis is to find the one true soul who loves him or her enough to pass Artemis's test. That person must take the medallion that contains the Dark-Hunter's soul and hold it to the bow-and-arrow mark on the Dark-Hunter's body until the soul returns. The medallion is lava-hot and will scar the hand. If the person can't maintain his or her grip and the medallion is dropped, the soul is released into nothing. This traps the Dark-Hunter into a painful existence as a Shade. If, on the other hand, the lover succeeds, the Dark-Hunter is once again a mortal with a soul, restarting life at the age they were when they first died.

Dark-Hunter Code: Honor Artemis. Drink no blood. Harm no human or Apollite. Never touch your Squire. Speak with no family, no friends who knew you before you died. Let no Daimon escape alive. Never speak of what you are. You walk alone. Keep your bow mark hidden.

Dark-Hunter.com: An online community of Dark-Hunters and Squires disguised as a fiction and role-play Web site.

Dayslayer: Apollite myth of a Daimon/Apollite who can walk in daylight. (See **Thanatos**.)

Desiderius: Dangerous demigod Spathi Daimon with a grudge against the Devereaux family. Appears in *Seize the Night* and *Night Pleasures*. Can control minds and throw bolts of lightning.

Devereaux: A close-knit family of sisters with a lot of magical talent. Daughters include Esmerelda (Essie);

Yasmina (Mina); Petra; Ekaterina (Trina); Karma; Tiyana (Tia)—a voodoo princess; Selena (Lane)—a psychic; Tabitha (Tabby)—a human Vampire-Hunter; and Amanda—an accountant. (See also **Devereaux, Tabitha**; **Hunter, Amanda**; and **Laurens, Bill and Selena**.)

Devereaux, Tabitha: A member of the Devereaux family who hunts Daimons. Owns Pandora's Box, an adult shop on Bourbon Street. Has the ability to sense others' emotions, a quick temper, and an unmatched vibrancy. Twin sister to Amanda Hunter and wife of Valerius Magnus.

Dionysus: Greek god of wine and excess—now amuses himself as a corporate raider. Usually appears as a tall man with short brown hair and a neat goatee. Appears in *Night Embrace*. Not a very good driver . . .

Divine, Marla: Drag queen friend of Tabitha Devereaux. Loves to steal men's coats. Was once escorted in a drag pageant by a very uptight Dark-Hunter.

Dorean Squires: Dorean Squires don't serve a particular Dark-Hunter, but rather serve the whole group. These Squires set up businesses that fulfill the more bizarre needs of the Dark-Hunters such as making specialized weapons or cars. They are also bankers and lawyers who know all about the Dark-Hunter world and who help keep up the appearance of normality.

Doulos: A human servant of Apollites and Daimons.

Dream-Hunters: Dream-Hunters are the children of the Greek gods of sleep. Some of them are born of human mothers, but most are born of the Greek goddess Mist.

Dream-Hunters are also known as Oneroi. Long ago, one of the Oneroi played a trick on the Greek god Zeus. In anger, the god cursed all of their kind to have no emotion whatsoever. Now the only time they can feel anything is when they are in a human's dreams.

Because this is seductive, Oneroi may only visit dreams; they may never participate and never revisit the same human.

There are also a few Dream-Hunters who prefer to stay out of dreams, except to police their own brethren. All Dream-Hunters take a prefix to their name so that everyone will know their role:

M' are the enforcers, they work like a police force and are the leaders.

V' are the ones who help humans who are having trouble sleeping or who have nightmares.

D' are the ones who help the gods and immortals. One of these is almost always sent in to aid newly created Dark-Hunters. Since the Dark-Hunters usually come from horrible pasts, they tend to be plagued with nightmares. Their designated Dream-Hunter will usually watch over them throughout their entire DH existence.

The Dream-Hunter world is complex, but not hard to understand. The main thing to remember is that they are born gods or half-gods. They can be either male or female, and for the most part, they leave the human realm alone and are found only in your wildest dreams as lovers or demons.

Sometimes a Dream-Hunter will become enamored of a dreamer. Sometimes they even instigate the dreams and alter them to enhance their borrowed emotions. When this happens, they are termed Skoti. Oneroi are charged with seeking them out to punish them for their actions.

However, many of the Skoti go unchecked and un-caught. They inhabit our dreams as incubi and succubi.

Eda: Archon's sister, Atlantean Earth goddess.
Elekti: Atlantean word meaning "chosen."

Elysia: A secret underground Apollite city, where Apollites live hidden from humans and Daimons alike. One of the oldest Apollite cities in North America. Home to Phoebe Peters. Featured in *Kiss of the Night*.

Eriksson, Christopher (Chris) Lars: Wulf Tryggvason's Squire and a direct descendant of Wulf's brother. Since Chris is the sole surviving member of Wulf's family, he is the only human who can remember Wulf and who he is.

Eros and Psyche: Married Greek gods of sexual desire and the soul. Often seen playing pool and poker at Sanctuary.

Eycharistisi: Atlantean word for "pleasure." Also a potent Atlantean aphrodisiac that floods the body with endorphins and destroys all inhibitions.

Gallagher, Jamie: Gangster Dark-Hunter from the American Prohibition era. Killed when he fell in love and tried to go straight. Featured in "A Dark-Hunter Christmas."

Gataki: Term of endearment, meaning "kitten."

Gautier, Cherise: Nick Gautier's mother, who had him when she was only fifteen. A beautiful, kindhearted woman in her early forties who works at Sanctuary.

Gautier, Nicholas (Nick) Ambrosius: Kyrian's Squire. A young man with a rough past, a loving mother, and an irreverent attitude. Nick is fiercely loyal and as close to being a friend of Acheron's as any mortal can be.

Gilbert: Valerius Magnus's trusted servant and butler, who would like to be a Squire.

Hold the human hair: A phrase used at Sanctuary to indicate that a Were-Hunter wants an especially strong drink, one that would inebriate a human with one shot.

Weres have a higher metabolism and can handle a lot more alcohol.

Hunter, Amanda: One of the Devereaux sisters, Amanda always wanted to be more normal than the empaths, voodoo priestesses, and psychics she was raised with. Tabitha Devereaux is her twin sister. Amanda became an accountant, but the supernatural found her anyway. Heroine of *Night Pleasures*, she is a human sorceress, married to Kyrian Hunter, and the mother of Marissa Hunter.

Hunter, Kyrian: Ancient Greek Dark-Hunter. Born prince and heir to Thrace, Kyrian was disinherited when he married an ex-prostitute against his father's wishes. As a legendary Macedonian general, he cut a trail of slaughter through the Mediterranean during the Fourth Macedonian War. Chroniclers wrote that he would break the Roman stranglehold on the known world and claim Rome for his own. He would have succeeded had he not been betrayed by his wife and delivered into the hands of his enemies. He was tortured for weeks and then executed by Valerius's grandfather. Hero of *Night Pleasures*. He is the husband of Amanda Hunter and father of Marissa Hunter.

Hunter, Marissa: Amanda and Kyrian Hunter's daughter, Marissa is a baby with astounding powers and a favorite with Acheron and Simi.

Hypnos: Greek God who holds dominion over all the gods of sleep.

I am the Light of the Lyre: Phrase used by Daimons and Apollites to seek shelter from another Daimon or Apollite. Refers to their kinship to Apollo, god of the sun.

Ias of Groesia: An ancient Greek Dark-Hunter. One of

the first three created, along with Callabrax and Kyros. Cruelly betrayed by his wife.

Icelus: Greek god who creates human shapes in dreams, and father of some Dream-Hunters. His children tend to be the more erotic Dream-Hunters. They live for sex and drift from dream to dream seeking new partners.

Idios: A rare serum made by the Oneroi that allows the user to become one with the dreamer for a short time. Used in dreams to guide and direct, allowing one sleeper to experience another's life so he can better understand it.

Illuminati: The Spathi Daimon bodyguards of Apollymi, led by Stryker and comprising between thirty and forty members. They include the oldest and most powerful of the Spathi.

Inferno: Also known as Dante's Inferno. The nightclub run by Dante Pontis, located in Minnesota.

Inkblot: A derogatory term for Daimons stemming from the strange black mark that all Daimons develop on their chests when they cross over from being Apollites to human slayers. This is what a dagger or sharp object must pierce to kill a Daimon.

Kallinos, Jasyn: A Katagaria Were-Hunter, Jaysn changes into a hawk. He is one of Sanctuary's deadlier inhabitants.

Kallitechnis: A Greek term meaning "dream master."

Kalosis: Atlantean word for "hell." The place where Apollymi is imprisoned so that she can see the human world but not participate in it. It is also where the Spathi Daimons live in perpetual darkness. No Dark-Hunter can enter and few Were-Hunters are allowed to live after visiting this realm, but it is accessible to Daimons through bolt-holes or laminas.

Katagaria: See **Were-Hunters.**

Katoteros: The Atlantean term for "heaven," and where Acheron makes his home. All Apollites and Daimons dream of being able to reclaim their right to rest here.

Kattalakis: A family name that indicates direct descent from one of King Lycaon's sons. The name belongs to the Drakos and Lykos branches on both the Arcadian and Katagaria side. Family members include Vane, Fang, Fury, Sebastian, Damos, Makis, Illarion, Bracis, Acmenis, Antiphone, Percy, Markos, Dare, Bryani, and Star, among many others.

Kattalakis, Bryani: An Arcadian Lykos Were-Huntress; mother to Vane, Fang, Anya, Fury, Dare, and Star. She has three vicious-looking scars on her face and neck and is a Sentinel. Bryani dresses like something out of a *Xena* episode. She hates Vane and his Katagaria father who tried to force her to accept him as mate. Lives in Dark Age Britain.

Kattalakis, Fang: A Katagari Were-Hunter who changes into a brown timber wolf. Fang loves to crack bad jokes and is currently recuperating from wounds under the care of Aimee Peltier at Sanctuary. Brother of Vane and Fury.

Kattalakis, Fury: Vane's littermate. Like Vane, he is a large white timber wolf in animal form, with a distinguishing brown spot. Fury was born in human form and was Arcadian until puberty when his Katagari half took over.

Kattalakis, Markus: Katagari Were-Hunter. Changes into a brown timber wolf. Tried to force Bryani to accept him as mate and failed. Father of Vane, Fang, and Fury, among others.

Kattalakis, Sebastian: Arcadian Drakos Were-Hunter, grandson of King Lycaon. Was excommunicated from his patria after the death of his sister. Now he walks as a solitary Sentinel, and has done so for four hundred years. Hero of "Dragonswan (*Tapestry*)."

Kattalakis, Vane: Arcadian Were-Hunter. He is a large, solid white timber wolf in animal form. Vane was born Katagaria but changed to Arcadian when puberty gave him his magic and his human form. He was protected from his pack by his brother Fang and his sister Anya. Vane is an Aristo and a Sentinel. Brother of Anya, Fang, and Fury. Hero of *Night Play*.

Kell: A former Roman gladiator from Dacia, now a Dark-Hunter stationed in Dallas. Makes weapons for the Dark-Hunters.

Kori: Handmaiden to Artemis, the most noted of which is Kat Agrotera.

Kouti, Pandora: Heroine of "Winter Born (*Stroke of Midnight*)," Arcadian were-pantheress. Pandora is of a patria whose women are subject to a bargain with a Katagaria panther patria, but she is not willing to honor it—she will fight back. Pandora is mated to Katagaria panther Dante Pontis.

Kyklonas: A ceredon guarding Apollymi's temple in Kalosis. Its name means "tornado."

Kyrios: A respectful Atlantean term for "lord."

Kyros of Seklos: An ancient Greek Dark-Hunter. One of the first three created, along with Callabrax and Ias. Stationed in Aberdeen, Mississippi.

Lachesis: The middle of the Three Fates, responsible for weaving the pattern of fate. Sister to Astrid and daughter of Themis. Also known as Lacy.

Laminas: Atlantean term for "haven." It can refer to a portal between Kalosis and the human world, often used by Spathi Daimons, that is also known as a bolt-hole.

This term is also applied to any Were-Hunter sanctuary. These are established safe houses where the Were-Hunters can go without fear of being hunted by their own kind. Apollites and Daimons in those havens are safe from Dark-Hunters.

Laurens, Bill and Selena: Bill is a politically connected lawyer, who sometimes does work for the Dark-Hunters, but his real ties are to the Were-Hunters. His wife, Selena, is a psychic who tells fortunes in Jackson Square in New Orleans. Selena is a Devereaux sister, and the best friend of Grace Alexander. In fact, Selena is the one who gave Grace the enchanted book at the beginning of *Fantasy Lover*. She is impulsive and emotional—the perfect foil for Bill.

Liza: A Dorean Squire who owns a doll shop on Royal Street in New Orleans. She makes custom dolls and special weapons for the Dark-Hunters.

Loki: The Norse trickster god.

Lycaon: The king who used his magic to make the Were-Hunter races.

MacRae, Channon: A history professor at the University of Virginia specializing in pre-Norman Britain. Heroine of "Dragonswan (*Tapestry*)."

M'Adoc: An Oneroi Dream-Hunter, he is the son of Phantasos. He is an Enforcer who watches over both the Oneroi and the Skoti. He is quick to issue orders, but seldom takes them. M'Adoc is the Oneroi of last resort. When he comes after you, you know you're going to pay. He often takes the jobs no one else wants to do.

Magnus, Valerius: A Dark-Hunter from ancient Rome, Valerius was once the son of a Roman senator. As a Roman general, he led conquests throughout Greece, Gaul, and Britannia. He doesn't play well with most

Dark-Hunters, since so many come from Greece or other countries he conquered. Val is truly ostracized from the rest of his brethren. He is very formal and currently posted in New Orleans. He is the half-brother of Zarek and hero of *Seize the Night*.

Marvin the Monkey: Sanctuary's mascot, Marvin is the only *real* animal in Sanctuary. Good friends with Wren Tigarian.

McDaniels, Erin: Corporate drone who has repressed her more creative impulses and thus is a prime target for Skoti. Heroine of "Phantom Lover (*Midnight Pleasures*)."

McTierney: A human family with connections to the Were-Hunter world. Members include mother Joyce, father Paul, and children Bride, Dierdre, and Patrick. Paul is a veterinarian famous around the New Orleans area for his ads promoting neutering. The family have several pets: Titus, a black rottweiler; the Professor and Marianne, two cats; Bart, a gator; and a rotating cast of recuperating animals.

McTierney, Bride: A human who owns the Lilac and Lace Boutique on Iberville in the French Quarter. She lives in an apartment behind her shop and is the heroine of *Kiss of the Night*.

Metriazo collar: A thin silver collar that sends tiny ionic pulses into the body of a Were-Hunter to prevent him or her from using their magic powers.

M'gios: The Atlantean word for "my son."

M'Ordant: Oneroi Dream-Hunter, son of Phantasos, he is an Enforcer who watches over both the Oneroi and the Skoti. He is hard-nosed and down-to-business. Still, he has a degree of compassion that is forbidden to his kind. It doesn't stop him from doing whatever is necessary to do his job. He makes his appearance in "Phantom Lover (*Midnight Pleasures*)."

Morginne: A Dark-Huntress who tricked Wulf Tryggva-son into trading souls and cursed him so that no human except one of his bloodline can remember him.

Morpheus: Greek god of dreams; father of many Oneroi.

Morrigan: The Celtic Raven goddess. Talon swore loy-alty to her during his human lifetime, but she seemed to have abandoned him long before his death. She is the grandmother of Sunshine Runningwolf.

Mount Olympus: Home of the Greek gods.

Nynia: Talon's first love, during his human lifetime. She was an ancient Celt, and a fisherman's daughter whom Talon insisted upon marrying despite the clan's disap-proval. She died giving birth to his stillborn child.

Nyx: Greek goddess of night.

Omegrion: The ruling council of the Were-Hunters. Sim-ilar to a senate, one representative from each branch of the Arcadian and Katagaria is sent to represent them all. They make laws that govern all the Were-Hunters and are responsible for setting up sanctuaries. A = Ar-cadian representative, K = Katagaria representative.

Its members are: Litarian (lions) Patrice Leonides (A), Paris Sebastienne (K); Drakos (dragons) Damos Kattalakis (A), Darion Kattalakis (K); Gerakian (hawks, falcons, and eagles) Arion Petrakis (A), Draven Hawke (K); Tigarian (tigers) Adrian Gavril (A), Lysander Stephanos (K); Lykos (wolves) Vane Kattalakis (A), Fury Kattalakis (K); Ursulan (bears) Leo Apollonian (A), Nicolette Peltier (K); Panthiras (panthers) Alexan-der James (A), Dante Pontis (K); Tsakalis (jackals) Constantine (A), Vincenzo Moretti (K); Niphetos Pardalia (snow leopards) Anelise Romano (A), Wren Tigarian (K); Pardalia (leopards) Dorian Kontis (A),

Stefan Kouris (K); Balios (jaguars) extinct (A), Myles
Stephanopoulos (K); Helikias (cheetahs) Jace Wilder
(A), Michael Giovanni (K).

Oneroi: Dream-Hunters responsible for watching over
human dreams and protecting them from Skoti. Often
assigned to newly created Dark-Hunters to heal them
mentally.

Oracle: Anyone who communes with the gods.

Orasia: The Atlantean goddess of sleep.

Ouisa: Distinct from the body and the soul, the Ouisa is
the personality—the part of a person that is left when a
Dark-Hunter becomes a Shade.

Parthenopaeus, Acheron (Ash): Ancient immortal Atlantean, leader of the Dark-Hunters. Born in 9548 B.C.
on the Greek isle of Didymos to King Acarion and
Queen Aara. His promises and curses are binding and
can have unintended consequences. Tall and naturally
blond, he dyes his hair different colors and dresses like
a Goth most of the time. He looks about twenty-one
and makes his home in Katoteros.

No one knows anything about him and he likes it
that way. In reality, he is a god-killer and an Atlantean
god with powers that no one knows the full extent of.
He refuses to answer any personal questions and he
must keep his word no matter what. The correct At-
lantean/Greek pronunciation of his name is *Ack-uh-
rahn Pahr-thin-oh-pay-us*. These days, only the older
Dark-Hunters and Artemis pronounce it that way. The
rest either call him Ash or *Ash-uh-rahn*. The exceptions to this are his demon, Simi, who calls him akri,
and Talon, who calls him T-Rex.

Patria: A family grouping of Were-Hunters of the same
race and animal genus.

Peltier: The family of bear Katagaria Were-Hunters who run the Sanctuary bar in New Orleans. Family members include Nicolette, Aubert, Dev, Kyle, Aimee, Remi, Quinn, Zar, Serre, Etienne, Alain, Cody, Griffe, and Cherif. Mama (Nicolette) and Papa (Aubert) Bear decided to found Sanctuary as a safe zone after their cubs Bastien and Gilbert were brutally killed by Arcadian Sentinels.

Peltier House: Adjacent to the bar, Peltier House is the living quarters for Sanctuary's hidden animal population. There they can assume their animal forms without fear of discovery and their young cubs are protected. It has more alarms than Fort Knox and is always guarded by at least two Peltier family members.

Peters, Cassandra Elaine: Half human and half Apollite, she is one of the last Apollites in the direct bloodline of Apollo. Daughter of Jefferson and sister to Phoebe and Nia. The Peters family is subject to a prophecy that if they all die, the Apollites will be free of their curse, so they are hunted by Spathi Daimons who want their freedom. The truth, however, is that if their bloodline dies out, so does the earth and all who live here. Heroine of *Kiss of the Night*.

Peters, Jefferson T.: Cassandra and Phoebe Peters's human father. Wealthy owner and founder of one of the world's largest pharmaceutical research and development companies.

Peters, Nia: Cassandra's sister and Jefferson's half-Apollite daughter. One of the last direct descendants of Apollo. Died with her mother when Spathi Daimons blew up their car.

Peters, Phoebe: Cassandra's sister and Jefferson's half-Apollite daughter. One of the last direct descendants of Apollo. She was rescued from the Spathi attack that killed her mother and sister Nia. After their deaths, Urian turned her Daimon. Lives in Elysia as Urian's wife.

Phantasos: Greek god who creates nonsentient dream objects, father of some Dream-Hunters. His children tend to be more cerebral and they are most often the Oneroi who police the Dream-Hunters.

Phaser: An Arcadian Sentinel weapon developed for use against the Katagaria. Stronger than a Taser, it sends a vicious jolt of electricity through the victims, causing their magic to go berserk. They are unable to hold either of their forms and a strong enough jolt will cause them to literally fall out of their bodies and become noncorporeal beings such as ghosts.

Phobetor: God of animal shapes, father of some of the Dream-Hunters. Phobetor's children tend to make nightmares. They often take the shapes of demons, dragons, and other terrifying images.

Pontis: A patria of Katagaria Were-Panthers. Includes Dante, Romeo, Michelangelo (Mike), Leonardo (Leo), Gabriel, Angel, Donatello, Bonita, Sal, and Tyla, among others.

Pontis, Dante: A Katagari Panther who owns Dante's Inferno in the Twin Cities, Minnesota. Though he technically owns one of the known Were-Hunter sanctuaries, he's not nearly as tolerant as other sanctuary owners. He is the head of his family and tends to take no crap from anyone. He first appears in *Kiss of the Night*, is the hero of "Winter Born (*Stroke of Midnight*)," and is mated to the Arcadian panther Pandora Koutis.

Priapus: Greek and Roman sex god, half brother of Julian Alexander.

Regis: Leader of a Were-Hunter pack who is essentially their king and representative.

Rogue Dark-Hunter: One who has breached the Dark-Hunter Code and must die. Hunted by Blood Rite Squires or Thanatos.

Runningwolf, Sunshine: Daughter of Starla and Daniel. A free spirit and an artist of tremendous talent who is easily distracted from the practical. Sells her art in Jackson Square and likes the color pink. Heroine of *Night Embrace* and now married to Talon Runningwolf.

Runningwolf, Talon: An ancient Celtic Dark-Hunter known as Speirr (which meant "Talon" in his language) in his human life. He was the son of a Druid high priest and a Celtic queen, and was high chieftain of his clan. After the deaths of his aunt, uncle, wife, and son over a short period of time, he was told that his ancient gods had cursed him. To appease the gods, he allowed himself to be sacrificed. Once his clan had Talon secured to the altar, they killed his sister before his eyes and then turned on him. As a Dark-Hunter, Talon has the power of telekinesis. He walks between this realm and the next with the help of Spirit Guides, and loses power when he feels negative emotions. The hero of *Night Embrace* and married to Sunshine Runningwolf.

Runningwolf's: A club on Canal Street in New Orleans run by Starla and Daniel Runningwolf.

Ryssa: A Greek princess who was one of Apollo's favorite mistresses. She bore him a son, which led the Apollite queen to such jealousy that she sent a team of Apollites to kill them. They were ordered to make it look like an animal had done it. That act caused Apollo to curse all the Apollites.

Rytis: An invisible stream of waves that move through everything. The waves echo, flow, and occasionally buckle. The Rytis is what Were- and Dream-Hunters use to move through space and time.

Saga: The Norse goddess of poetry.

Sanctuary: The premier New Orleans biker bar, owned by the Peltiers, a clan of Katagaria bears. It is a laminas: a safe zone for all types of Hunters where natural rivalries are put aside and no fighting or killing is allowed.

Santana, Wayne: Convicted and imprisoned for involuntary manslaughter while still young, Wayne lucked out when the Runningwolf family decided to hire him despite his record. They lucked out, too, in gaining a faithful friend and a good lookout for absentminded Sunshine.

Sasha: Astrid's Katagari Were-Hunter companion in *Dance with the Devil*. He's a large white timber wolf in animal form and a lot of attitude in any form.

Savitar: Even more mysterious than Acheron, he is rumored to have been the one to train Ash in his powers. He oversees the Omegrion even though none of the Were-Hunters are sure hów this came about. He has a strong fascination for the beach and surfing, and is usually found dressed as a surfer or beach bum. No one, not even Acheron, knows anything at all about him. He is extremely powerful and deadly. Most of his body is covered with tattoos.

Sentinels: Out of the Arcadian patrias are born the Sentinels—the Guardians of man- and were-kind. Only a select few are born to each patria. They are the strongest Were-Hunters and they pursue and execute Slayers. A colorful geometric design covers one side of an Arcadian Sentinel's face once they reach maturity, but the Sentinel can hide the design if he or she chooses.

Sfora: A scrying globe that people in Katoteros can use to watch events in other realms, including the human realm. Sometimes those being viewed can sense that sŏmeone is watching.

Shade: What a Dark-Hunter becomes when he is killed and does not immediately get invested with a soul. Shadedom is an existence of unrelenting hunger and thirst, but its worst aspect is that the Shade is invisible to all mortals and denied contact with everyone—so it quickly goes insane screaming for attention in its solitary confinement. There are rumors of an out clause for Shades.

Simi: Acheron's Charonte demon, who can manifest as a human or a demon, and who rests as an ever-changing tattoo on Ash's body. Though she is thousands of years old, she is equivalent to a human eighteen-year-old. She is like a daughter to Acheron. Loves barbecue, movies, and QVC. Hates to be told no.

Also, the Charonte term for "baby."

Skoti: Usually the children of Phobetor, but can be any Dream-Hunter who goes bad. Nightmare demons· who infiltrate the dreams of humans to suck emotions and creativity from them, they are also incubi and succubi who derive sexual pleasure from their dream-hosts.

Slayer: Katagaria Were-Hunters driven to madness at puberty when they come into their powers, but fail to find a way to control them. They become ruthless slayers who kill anything or anyone who cross them. Similar to rabies, it is an infection for which there is no cure. Hunted by Sentinels.

Smith, Janice: An African-American Dark-Huntress with a Carribbean accent. Currently posted in New Orleans.

Spathi: Warrior Daimons. Apollymi's guards and pets, who can be reincarnated after they die if someone cares enough; their essence remains intact. See also **Illuminati**.

Squires: To help the Dark-Hunters appear "normal," Acheron set up a Squire's Council of humans who serve them. A Squire works with a Dark-Hunter, usually living in the same house, and—to the outside world—appearing to be the owner. It is a Squire's job to attend to all the day-to-day monotony of running the household so the Dark-Hunter can focus on killing Daimons. Squires are often at risk since the Daimons know a Squire is an emotional attachment for the Dark-Hunter.

　　If a Dark-Hunter is in danger, it is the Squire's responsibility to pull him or her out, although the Squire doesn't have immortality or psychic abilities. Like the Dark-Hunters they serve, they are extremely well paid for their services. (See also **Dorian Squires**, **Blue Blood Squires**.)

Strati: Term used for Katagaria soldiers who seek out Arcadians to fight. They are the Katagaria equivalent to Sentinels except they have no facial markings.

Strykerius (Stryker): The leader and trainer of Apollymi's Spathi Daimons and leader of the elite Illuminati force. He is the son of Apollo and turned on his father after Apollo cursed him and his race. He is the adopted son of Apollymi and father to Urian. Holds a grudge against Acheron and plots the deaths of all whom Ash holds dear.

Styxx: Acheron's human brother, and an identical twin. Styxx was born in 9548 B.C. on the Greek isle of Didymos to King Acarion and Queen Aara. His and Acheron's life forces are connected, so he can't die until Acheron does. Styxx has spent centuries hating Ash.

Summoning, the: A Daimon homing beacon the Dayslayer

can use to summon Daimons and Apollites to conference or for war.

Sundown: Sundown is a Dark-Hunter from the nineteenth-century American West. His real name is William Jessup "Jess" Brady. Jess was orphaned at age five and grew up under the harsh hand of a preacher man who owned the local orphanage. At eleven, he ran away and headed out West where he quickly learned life wasn't fair and it wasn't easy for a boy with no family. At sixteen, he was making his living as a gunslinger, train robber, and cardsharp. He lived his life hard and was ruthlessly shot in the back on his way to his wedding by his best man—the only man he'd ever trusted—who wanted to collect the bounty on his head. He is currently stationed in Reno, Nevada.

Swain: Suffix for a male Were-Hunter, e.g., dragonswain, pantherswain, bearswain, etc.

Swan: Suffix for a female Were-Hunter, e.g., dragonswan, pantherswan, bearswan, etc.

"Sweet Home Alabama": The Lynyrd Skynyrd song played to warn everyone in Sanctuary when Acheron comes into the bar.

Sword of Cronus: Julian Alexander's sword. Only those with the blood of Cronus in their veins may touch it without being burned.

Talpinas: At one time, a type of Squire whose sole purpose was to take care of Dark-Hunters' carnal needs. Long since banned by Artemis.

Tartarus: Greek version of hell. The realm where humans are punished for the sins of their lifetimes.

Tessera: A group of four Were-Hunters sent out to hunt others of their kind.

Thanatos: The Greek word for "death." Also, an Apollite

to whom Artemis gives special powers and whom he sends to kill rogue Dark-Hunters. Known as the Dayslayer in Apollite mythology. There has been more than one Thanatos over the centuries. See also **Callyx.**

Themis: Redheaded Greek goddess of justice, mother of Astrid and the Fates.

Theodorakopolus, Colt: A Were-Hunter Acadian Sentinel, Colt was orphaned at birth and raised at Sanctuary. Colt hides his Sentinel birthmark.

Theti Squires: The Squire police force that makes sure all Squires obey the laws. Unlike the Blood Rite Squires, they are not allowed to kill.

Thirio: The need Were-Hunters feel when mated to combine their life forces so if one dies, they both die. Can be resisted.

Thrylos: Greek word for "legend."

Tigarian, Wren: A Katagari Were-Hunter who can turn into a white tiger, a snow leopard, or a combination of the two. He has lived at Sanctuary since his parents died mysteriously violent deaths. He busses tables there and is extremely dangerous and withdrawn. He has no prejudice—he hates everyone and everything equally. His only friend is Nick and he will only interact peacefully with Aimee and Marvin.

Tree of Life: Supernatural tree that blooms only in the garden of the Atlantean Destroyer. Its leaves alone can break the ypnsi.

T-Rex: Talon's favorite irreverent nickname for Acheron.

Tryggvason, Erik: Son of Cassandra and Wulf and a direct descendant of Apollo. Guarded carefully and loved by too many protective males: Wulf, Chris, and Urian.

Tryggvason, Wulf: A Dark-Hunter Viking warrior whose recklessness brought him into contact with Morginne, a powerful Dark-Huntress. She tricked him into trading souls with her. He is the only Dark-Hunter who was never granted an Act of Vengeance. And since he was wrongfully brought over by another Dark-Hunter, his powers are very different from those of the rest of his brethren. The most curious power of all is that of amnesia. No human or animal is capable of remembering him five minutes after they leave his presence. The only exceptions to that are those who bear his blood. Hero of *Kiss of the Night*, husband of Cassandra Peters, and father of Erik Tryggvason. His soul is held by Loki.

Urian: A reincarnated Spathi Daimon, formerly Stryker's eldest and last surviving son, a former member of the Illuminati, and husband to Phoebe Peters. Stryker killed Phoebe and cut Urian's throat for helping Cassandra Peters, and since then, Urian has been an occasional and prickly ally of Acheron and the Dark-Hunters.

V'aiden: A Dream-Hunter who longs to feel. Hero of "Phantom Lover (*Midnight Pleasures*)."

Villkatt: An old Norse endearment meaning "wild cat."

Were-Hunters: An ancient Greek king (Lycaon) unknowingly married an Apollite. She hid what she was from him until her twenty-seventh birthday, when she perished painfully. When the king realized what she was, he also realized that their two sons would follow in their mother's footsteps and die horribly at age twenty-seven.

To prevent this, the king rounded up Apollites and began experimenting on them. He magically spliced their life forces with those of various animals (lions, dragons, birds of prey, tigers, wolves, bears, panthers, jackals, leopards, jaguars, and cheetahs) to create hybrid beings.

The splicing created two classes of beings: Arcadians, those who held human hearts and could shapeshift into animals, and Katagaria, those who had animal hearts and could become human.

Once the king was done experimenting, he chose the two most powerful creatures (wolves and dragons) and merged them with his own children. When the Greek Fates saw this, they were angered that he would dare to try to thwart them. They demanded he kill his sons and all the others he had created.

He refused.

As punishment, the Fates decreed that the two species would always war against each other. The Arcadians and the Katagaria would never know peace. To this day and beyond, they hunt each other and wage their war.

Unlike their Apollite cousins, they live for hundreds of years. They share the same psychic abilities as the Apollites, plus they have a few extra abilities such as time travel and the ability to shapeshift.

Were-Hunter patrias are: Litarian (lions); Drakos (dragons); Gerakian (hawks, falcons, and eagles); Tigarian (tigers); Lykos (wolves); Ursulan (bears); Panthiras (panthers); Tsakalis (jackals); Niphetos Pardalia (snow leopards); Pardalia (leopards); Balios (jaguars); Helikias (cheetahs).

Were-Hunter Mate: Each Were-Hunter has a mate that is chosen, usually against their wills, by the Fates. Mates are indicated by a special matching tattoo that appears on the hand of both partners a few hours after they have sex. They then have three weeks to accept or reject the pairing. There is no way to force one

partner to accept the other. If the mating is mutually
accepted, they can have children together. If not, both
will be sterile for the rest of their lives. After finding
his mate, a male Were-Hunter will never be able to have
sex with anyone else again. A female Were-Hunter will
be able to have sex, but won't be able to have children
with anyone else. (See also **Thirio**.)

Whitethunder, Carson: An Arcadian Were-Hunter who
changes into a hawk, Carson is the resident vet and
medical doctor at Sanctuary. He goes to Dr. Paul Mc-
Tierney for advice on particularly tricky animal cases.

Wink: A minor Greek god of sleep, son of Nyx and Ere-
bus. His mist can be used by a Dream-Hunter to make
a human drowsy or to exert control over one. V'aiden's
great-uncle.

Ydor: Atlantean ocean god.

Ypnsi: Sacred sleep that Orasia had once dispensed from
the sacred halls of Katoteros, back in the days when the
ancient Atlantean gods ruled the earth.

Zarek of Moesia: A Dark-Hunter who was born the un-
wanted son of a Greek slave and a Roman senator. Moments after his birth, his mother gave him to a servant
with orders to kill the infant. The servant took mercy
on the child and took him to his father, who had no
more use for the baby than his mother. Thus Zarek became the whipping boy of a noble Roman family. He
trusts no one. He seldom interacts with other Dark-
Hunters, and when he does, it is always grudgingly
and with the utmost disdain for them. Because of his
steadfast refusal to follow any orders (even those of
Artemis) and his lack of regard for anyone other than
himself, he is kept in isolation in Alaska where his ac-
tivity is seriously limited and closely monitored. There

are many who fear he will one day unleash his powers against humans as well as Daimons. He is the hero of *Dance with the Devil* and married to Astrid.

Zurvan: Ancient Persian god of time and space. Also known as Cas.

Fantasy Lover

Julian of Macedon thinks that being trapped in a bedroom with a woman is a grand thing. But being trapped in hundreds of bedrooms over two thousand years isn't. And being cursed into a book as a love slave for eternity can ruin even a Spartan warrior's day. As a love slave, he knew everything about women. How to touch them, how to savor them, and most of all how to pleasure them. But when he was summoned to fulfill Grace Alexander's sexual fantasies, he found the first woman in history who saw him as a man with a tormented past. She alone bothered to take him out of the bedroom and into the world. She taught Julian to love again.

But he was cursed to walk eternity alone. And he's only allowed to stay with Grace for a month. For a chance to be together forever, they will have to fight a creepy stalker, jealous Greek gods, and their own desire for each other. Sure, love can heal all wounds, but can it break a two-thousand-year-old curse?

Night Pleasures

Kyrian of Thrace is immortal. He journeys through the night stalking the evil that preys on humans. He has unlimited wealth, unlimited power. Yes, his existence is dark and dangerous—he plays hero to thousands, but is known to none. And he loves every minute of it.

At least he does until one night when Kyrian wakes up handcuffed to his worst nightmare: a conservative woman in a button-down shirt. Or in Amanda's case, one buttoned all the way up to her chin. She's smart, sexy, witty, and wants nothing to do with the paranormal—in other words, him.

Kyrian's attraction to Amanda Devereaux goes against everything he stands for. Not to mention the last time he fell in love it cost him not only his human life, but also his very soul. Yet Amanda makes him want to try again. Want to believe that love and loyalty do exist.

Even more disturbing, can a woman like Amanda love a man whose battle scars run deep, and whose heart was damaged by a betrayal so savage that he's not sure it will ever beat again?

Night Embrace

Talon of the Morrigantes loves his immortality. He has chicory coffee, warm beignets, and his best friend on the cell phone. Once the sun goes down, he is the baddest thing prowling the night: He commands the elements, and knows no fear. All he wants in return is a hot babe in a red dress, just for the night.

Instead, Talon gets a runaway Mardi Gras float that tries to turn him into roadkill, and a beautiful woman who saves his life but can't remember where she put his pants. Flamboyant and extravagant, Sunshine Runningwolf should be the perfect woman for Talon. She wants nothing past tonight, no ties, no long-term commitments.

But just looking at her makes Talon yearn for dreams that he buried centuries ago. With her unconventional ways and ability to baffle, Sunshine is the one person he finds himself needing. But to love her would mean her death. Talon is cursed never to know peace or happiness—not so long as his enemy waits in the night to destroy them both.

Dance with the Devil

Zarek of Moesia doesn't get what's so great about being a Dark-Hunter. It's fine to be a soulless guardian standing between mankind and those who would see mankind destroyed. But the only benefit he has from his bargain is an eternity of solitude in Alaska. How thrilling.

One night nine hundred years ago, something happened. Something Zarek can't remember well. Something that got him exiled from his brethren. Now most other Dark-Hunters—and Artemis herself—think that Zarek has gone off the deep end from being alone too long. But after a lifetime as a Roman slave and nine centuries in exile, Zarek is tired of enduring hardship. He wants the truth about what happened the night he was exiled—he has nothing to lose and everything to gain.

Astrid is a justice nymph, a niece of Artemis sent down from Olympus to judge Zarek. An exceptional woman who can see straight to the truth, Astrid has never found anyone innocent. But she is brave enough to try to get to the truth behind Zarek's prickly façade. And when she smiles, his cold heart shatters.

They say even the most damned man can be forgiven. Zarek never believed that until the night Astrid opened her door to him and made him want to leave behind his inner feral beast to be human again. Made him want to love and be loved. But how can an ex-slave whose soul is owned by a Greek goddess ever dream of touching, let alone holding, a fiery star?

Kiss of the Night

What do you get when you have one immortal Viking warrior no one can remember five minutes after he leaves their presence, a princess on the run for her life, and one seriously annoyed demigod? Basically, you get Wulf Tryggvason's life.

It started out simple enough. One night Wulf went to save a woman in trouble. The next thing he knew, the doorway to hell had opened and out stepped Daimons—vampires the likes of which he'd never seen before. Led by the son of Apollo, they are out to end the curse that has banished them all to darkness. The only problem with that is they have to kill Cassandra Peters to do it, and if she dies, so dies the sun, the earth, and all who dwell here. Life's just a bowl full of cherries, ain't it?

Brought together by fate, it's now Wulf's job to protect a daughter of the very race he's been hunting for centuries. Neither of them dares to trust the other. But she is the only one who can remember him . . . More than that, with her courage and strength she is the only one who has ever reached a heart that he thought had died centuries ago.

The only way for a Dark-Hunter to regain his soul is through the love of a woman. But what happens when that woman isn't exactly human?

Night Play

Bride McTierney has had it with men. They're cheap, self-centered, and never love her for who she is. But though she prides herself on being independent, deep down she still yearns for a knight in shining armor.

She just never expected her knight in shining armor to have a shiny coat of fur . . .

Deadly and tortured, Vane Kattalakis isn't what he seems. Most women lament that their boyfriends are dogs. In Bride's case, hers is a wolf. A Were-Hunter wolf. Wanted dead by his enemies, Vane isn't looking for a mate. But the Fates have marked Bride as his. Now he has three weeks to either convince Bride that the supernatural is real or he will spend the rest of his life neutered—something no self-respecting wolf can accept . . .

But how does a wolf convince a human to trust him with her life when his enemies are out to end his? In the world of the Were-Hunters, it really is dog-eat-dog. And only one alpha male can win.

Seize the Night

Valerius Magnus was born the noble son of a legendary Roman senator. He walked through the ancient world as a general, admired and supreme until a brutal betrayal caused him to bargain his soul. Now he's an immortal Dark-Hunter, bound to protect mankind from the evil scourge that haunts it. Over the centuries, Valerius has seen many frightening things: plagues, pestilence, disco music . . .

And now Tabitha Devereaux. A human, she has trained herself to fight vampires every bit as capably as any Dark-Hunter. Idiosyncratic and off-beat, she is his personal bane—and yet she beguiles him. There are only two small problems. She happens to be the twin of his mortal enemy's wife. More than that, Tabitha and her sister are being stalked by a power that will not rest until everyone she holds dear is dead.

Unlike his Dark-Hunter brethren, Valerius relies on no one but himself. They spurned him, and he turned his back on them. But the only way to save Tabitha and her family is to find some way to bridge a two-thousand-year-old feud.

They say opposites attract, but can they stay together

when even the Fates conspire to keep them apart? Then again, the Fates have never dealt with the likes of Tabitha Devereaux before. They're going to be in for quite a fight . . .

Sins of the Night

In the realm of the Dark-Hunters, there is a code of honor that even immortal bad boys must follow: Harm no human. Drink no blood. Never fall in love.

But every now and again, a Dark-Hunter thinks himself above the Code. That is where Alexion comes in. Step over the line, and it's his wrath you face. Nothing can sway Alexion, or so he thought . . .

Then he met a female Dark-Hunter who goes by the name of Danger—it's not just her name, it's how she lives her life. She doesn't trust him at all. And who could blame her? She alone knows that Alexion is judge, jury, and, most likely, executioner of her friends. Yet she is his key to saving some of them. Without her, they will all die.

Dangereuse St. Richard is a deadly distraction. Something about her reawakens a heart he thought frozen forever. But in a race against evil, the only hope mankind has is for Alexion to do his duty. And how can he when it means that he will have to sacrifice the only woman he's ever loved?